A DELIGHTFUL DECEIT

ALEXA SANTI

Copyright © 2021 by Alexa Santi

All rights reserved.

Cover by Period Images and The Cover Fling

No part of this book may be reproduced in any form or by any electronic or mechanical means, including information storage and retrieval systems, without written permission from the author, except for the use of brief quotations in a book review.

JULY 1815

As Grace Rawson descended from her aunt's traveling coach, she had the oddest feeling she was being watched.

She looked around and saw no one. Not even so much as the twitch of a curtain at the drawing room window. *Ridiculous, of course.*

She must be feeling conspicuous because she had finally allowed Aunt Harriet to coax her out of the mourning dresses she had worn since her only brother and last close relative had been killed at Toulouse last spring. The light gray and lavender dresses of half-mourning were more flattering to her complexion, to be sure, but Grace had not definitely decided that she was ready to rejoin a social life despite Aunt Harriet's insistence.

Not hearing any sounds from within the coach, Grace turned and poked her head back inside.

Harriet's eyes were only just opening and she yawned widely as she stretched and sat up. "Are we here already?"

"Yes, Aunt Harriet," Grace said, and stepped back to allow the hovering footman to offer his hand so Harriet could descend. Harriet paused in the open door for a moment, shook out her skirts, and descended with a lively bounce that Grace could not help resenting.

Her aunt's ability to sleep anytime, anywhere, must have been an asset during the older woman's constant travels with her late husband, but in Grace's opinion it made Harriet a very dull traveling companion. Harriet took Grace's arm as Parker, her aunt's lady's maid, followed behind, her face set in its usual impassive lines.

"We are three hours late and likely to miss supper," Grace said, trying not to feel like her aunt's governess. "The rain slowed us even more than John Coachman thought it would."

Harriet clucked her tongue. "You must learn

to be more flexible, my dear. These little inconveniences are all a part of travelling."

Grace confined herself to a shake of her head as she followed in Harriet's wake. The butler opened the front door and bowed them inside as Lady Ashburton hurried into the hallway, her hands extended. The plumes in her hair bobbed and waved as she approached, making Grace think of a fancy chicken making its stately way across the barnyard. She bit her lip to suppress her smile, and curtseyed gravely to their hostess.

"My dear Harriet!"

"Catherine, so good to see you."

The two older women exchanged salutes on the cheek, and Lady Ashburton nodded cordially to Grace as Parker followed a young footman upstairs.

"Do say you will have supper with us, Harriet. I can put it back another half-hour." Lady Ashburton winked and nodded at Grace. "There is *someone* who is quite eager to see Miss Rawson this evening. He asked after her particularly."

Oh, Lord. Sir Malcolm must have arrived before them. That knowledge did not make Grace any more eager to attend supper, especially when both of the older ladies scrutinized her from head to toe, giggling like schoolgirls.

Harriet said, "Since you insist, Catherine, we accept. We shall change and be downstairs as quickly as we can."

"Are you sure you're feeling well enough, Aunt Harriet?" Grace said, trying not to grit her teeth. For at least the last hour of their journey, she had been looking forward to loosening her stays and sinking into a cozy, *non-moving* armchair.

Harriet waved her hand airily. "I feel perfectly well, and I am eager to meet the rest of the guests. Do hurry, Grace."

The worst part, Grace thought, was that Harriet probably *was* perfectly well. Grace was not yet thirty to Harriet's almost sixty years, but keeping up with the social whirlwind that was her aunt had proved more taxing than Grace imagined when she first accepted Harriet's invitation to be her companion. She certainly had not expected her aunt to announce they would attend *four* house parties in as many weeks this summer, with less than a week to prepare for their departure. The last of her new dresses had arrived only the evening before they left.

The footman tapped at the door of the room assigned to Harriet, and Parker opened it.

"Run along to your room, Grace, and I'll send Parker to you as soon as she is done helping me."

"Yes, madam," Parker said, with a distinct lack of enthusiasm in her voice.

Grace was not much more enthusiastic than Parker, but obediently followed the footman to nearly the end of the hallway, where he opened a door and bowed her in.

"I'll be right back with your trunk, miss."

As the door closed behind him, Grace plunked herself in a plush armchair and closed her eyes with a sigh. She wanted to remain by the fire like the old maid she was, but she couldn't possibly insult their hostess by not attending supper, not when Harriet was planning to go.

She was half-dozing by the time the footman returned with her small trunk, followed by a harried housemaid who immediately rifled through Grace's trunk so her evening dress could be hastily pressed before supper. As she waited, Grace washed away the worst of her travel dust before the maid hurried back in. The dress was another of the new ones Aunt Harriet had insisted on buying her, lavender silk with a silvery-gray overdress. It was half-mourning, but Grace felt more than a little conspicuous in it, especially once she realized the neckline was lower than any she had worn since her debut almost ten years before, and probably not even then. She tried not to feel like mutton dressed as lamb when Parker bustled in to do her hair.

Parker had no interest in helping Grace find a fichu to fill in the neckline, but sat her down on a stool and tugged her flyaway hair into a serviceable twist before all but pushing her out the door of her room. "You must hurry, miss, the other guests will be going in to supper at any moment."

Grace set her steps towards the drawing room, where the doors stood open to show people milling about inside. She heard Aunt Harriet's trilling laugh, but couldn't see her in the crowd.

"There you are at last, Miss Rawson," Lady Ashburton said, her voice carrying above the rest of the group, which quieted and turned as one to stare at Grace. "We have been waiting supper for you."

Grace felt her face flush to the roots of her hair, and bobbed a curtsey. "I am very grateful, Lady Ashburton."

A man appeared at Grace's elbow and bowed to her. She forced herself to smile at him.

"How good to see you, Sir Malcolm," she said, and he bowed over her hand.

"And I you, Miss Rawson."

Sir Malcolm Stewart wasn't *un*attractive, Grace supposed. He bathed regularly, he had all his teeth, and his hairline was only just beginning to recede as he approached the age of forty. He was a respected Member of Parliament and owned a prosperous estate in Kent. He was widely regarded as a catch in Aunt Harriet's social circle, which was one reason Grace found herself reluctant to discourage him entirely. As an impoverished spinster, marriage prospects were too few and far between for her to dismiss Sir Malcolm out of hand.

But there was something about him that made Grace wary, and she could not say precisely what it was. Something about the man made her feel she needed to be on her guard whenever they were in company together.

"Did you have a good journey?" he asked.

"Yes, thank you."

"And your aunt is well?"

"Yes, thank you."

And just like that, they were out of conversation. Fortunately, the butler entered to announce supper and Sir Malcolm extended his arm to escort her to her seat at the table and then depart for his own, a few places down and on the other side.

Once seated, Grace found herself far sleepier in the warm room than she had expected. She did her best to hide her yawns behind her napkin, but it was a near-run thing a few times. Only her position at the center of the table saved her from embarrassment, seated as she was far from any persons of distinction who could note her fatigue and comment on it. She had an elderly gentleman friend of Harriet's on one side and an imperious dandy on the other. The padded shoulders of the dandy's superfine evening coat stuck out at a ridiculous angle and blond curls tumbled over his brow in a conspicuously wind-blown manner even on this windless evening. He was fully absorbed in drawling at the woman on his other side while the man on Grace's left was similarly occupied, so she let herself sink into something of a haze until she was startled by a comment addressed to her by the dandy.

"How do you find Hampshire?"

"The same as always," Grace said, "with a map."

She immediately bit her tongue as the dandy

stared at her in astonishment. His eyes were a pale but indeterminate shade in the candlelight, and a light that puzzled her flickered deep in them before it vanished almost as soon as it had appeared.

"I beg your pardon," she said. "I am rather tired."

"Of course," he said with exactly the tone of bored politeness she expected from him. He immediately turned the topic to the weather. She gave the socially expected replies, as she had done so many times before, but couldn't help wondering how he would react if she surprised him again. Would he stand up and denounce her? Would he pointedly turn back to his other supper partner?

What, exactly, could he do, though?

It was a strangely freeing idea, that she need not worry what a gentleman thought of her so long as he did not think her a loose woman. After all, she was a spinster of mature years— she would be thirty soon. Why did she need to impress any man or make him think well of her, especially if she did not think well of him?

Even as she considered it, she was able to continue her bland commentary on the weather and the journey from London. There was a strange tension to their conversation, as though the dandy expected her to make another odd comment at any moment.

She didn't want to give him the satisfaction of confirming she was peculiar. And yet, at the same time ... could she make another crack in his composure with a new observation?

Really, Grace, she scolded herself. She must be even more tired than she thought if she was tempted to play flirtatious games with a man she had never met before.

The supper partner on the dandy's other side drew his attention away, and Grace turned to the elderly gentleman on her other side as he smiled at her. With him, she would have no desire to act out of character.

WHEN THE GENTLEMEN arrived in the drawing room after supper, Sir Malcolm once again made his way to her side. She smiled and hoped it was not too obvious she was ambivalent about his presence. He bowed and took the seat next to her on the settee.

Grace wondered what would happen if she made a pert remark to Sir Malcolm as she had to her supper partner. She suspected Sir

Malcolm would only exchange yet another pleasantry with her regardless of what her responses might be. He certainly never seemed to pay much attention to her replies despite the frequency with which he sought out her company. Even now, Sir Malcolm's gaze roamed the room as they discussed the weather and the journey and other commonplaces that required only the smallest portion of her attention.

She could see *him* across the room—the dandy. He drew her eye for reasons she did not want to understand. He was not at all the type of man she was interested in. Usually. He was clearly a man who spent the majority of his time gazing at his mirror to get his cravat just right.

Yet she had an odd sense he was observing the entire room even as he made polite conversation with the other guests, moving from group to group with languid grace.

"Do you know that man?" she asked Sir Malcolm.

He looked across the room with a slight frown. "He doesn't look familiar."

"He was one of my supper partners," she explained. "Unfortunately, we were not introduced before supper and I failed to catch his name."

Sir Malcolm shrugged. "He is likely a friend of Lord Dorchester's."

"Of course."

It made sense. Lord Dorchester was the eldest son of their host and a dandy himself, though the man across the room seemed to be a bit older, Grace's age or a few years her senior. Perhaps too old to still be exaggerating the sartorial tenets Brummell had set out so many years ago.

Though she had to admit, the look became him. Those broad shoulders were not all due to padding, and the requisite fawn-colored breeches hugged his—

"Miss Rawson?"

With a start, Grace looked at Sir Malcolm, who was frowning at her.

"I beg your pardon," she said. "My aunt and I had a long journey today, and I find I am more tired than I realized. I should excuse myself to our hostess."

"Not at all, Miss Rawson." He stood with her and bowed over her hand again. "I shall see you tomorrow."

She murmured a polite reply and went to make her apologies to Lady Ashburton and her aunt before leaving the room.

As she left, she felt that gaze again, the one

she had felt when they arrived. She glanced over her shoulder to catch the dandy turning his head away from her, as though he had been watching her until just that moment.

Nonsense. Grace shook her head as she mounted the stairs. Her exhaustion was leading her to be fanciful.

The next morning, Grace returned upstairs after an early breakfast and sat with her aunt as Harriet drank her morning tea and nibbled on a piece of toast. Harriet often took advantage of her advanced years to avoid having breakfast with the rest of the guests at a house party. She insisted that ten o'clock of the morning was far too early to make conversation with anyone but one's husband.

"Make sure you have your embroidery with you in the drawing room," Harriet said.

"Of course, Aunt Harriet. Is there anyone in particular you would like me to, er, listen in on?"

"That Miss Hawthorne," Harriet said positively. "She's a sly minx, and she's up to something. I want to know what it is."

"I'll do my best," Grace murmured. Early in their time together, Harriet had discovered Grace's role as her companion placed her in an ideal position to overhear the most entertaining bits of gossip once the other house party attendees forgot she was in the room. Plying her embroidery was one of the better ways to make herself invisible. Grace didn't mind—it gave her a purpose other than sitting in utter boredom. Constructing those pieces of gossip into an entertaining whole for Aunt Harriet made the time pass more quickly.

Grace smoothed the skirts of her lilac muslin dress as she rose from her chair. She usually depended on her mourning garb to make her invisible, but if Aunt Harriet insisted she wear half-mourning, Grace had no choice. She checked her hair with the other hand to make sure it had not escaped the lace-trimmed linen cap that held the unruly locks in place. The gentlemen were expected to join their host for grouse shooting that morning, so it was unlikely *he* would be there in any case.

Not that she cared.

Harriet frowned at her. "That cap is far too practical for that dress. And your nose has freckled again."

Grace resisted an urge to shield her nose from Harriet's critical gaze. "*You* insisted we go for that walk in Hyde Park even though I had forgotten my parasol."

"So I did. Well, Parker has the freckle lotion I bought for you. I'll just have her bring it to you before supper, shall I?"

Grace took a moment to tamp down her temper so she could smile at her aunt. "I wish you would not waste your money on that lotion, Aunt Harriet. All it does it make my nose peel, and that looks even worse than the freckles." She leaned down and kissed Harriet's cheek to forestall any further discussion of the matter. "I'll see you downstairs, shall I?"

Harriet took a last sip of her tea and nodded to her impassive maid. "You may let Lady Ashburton know I shall be down once Parker puts me to rights."

Picking up the netted bag that held her embroidery, Grace made her way downstairs, nearly as invisible as one of the servants as she approached the drawing room where the ladies were to gather that morning. To her surprise, several gentlemen dotted the room ... including the dandy from last night, who looked up as she entered the room. He had not been at breakfast, but seeing at the ornate folds of his cravat, she was not surprised. It must have taken him hours to create.

She would have thought his high collar points would prevent him from looking around the room, yet again she somehow had a sense he knew where everyone sat and who everyone was.

He was seated with their hostess, so she was forced to endure his insolent gaze once more as she crossed to Lady Ashburton to make her curtsy.

"Ah, Miss Rawson," her hostess said. "Did you sleep well?"

"Yes, I thank you, my lady," Grace said. Her room was probably the smallest one in the house that was still in the guest wing, with slightly shabby furnishings, but at least the mattress had been comfortable and the room free of drafts, which was more than she had had at other houses as her aunt's companion.

The dandy stood up from the settee and bowed to her.

"Have you met Mr. Parsloe? Mr. Parsloe, this is Miss Rawson."

He murmured something unintelligible and then re-seated himself, a clear dismissal. Grace glared at him, and his unreadable eyes met hers briefly. In the daylight, they were a strange, ambiguous shade of green—or gray?—that picked up some of the color of his dark blue coat.

Grace turned on her heel, still fuming, and looked around for Miss Hawthorne as inconspicuously as she could. She finally spotted her sitting near the unlit fireplace with a friend. Behind the two girls was an empty group of chairs that faced the window for the best light but was within easy earshot of their conversation. *Perfect.*

She knew she ought to concentrate on Miss Hawthorne, but Grace wasted several minutes fuming over the behavior of Mr. Parsloe, or whatever his name was, as she sorted through her silks. To re-seat himself while she was still standing in front of him! It was a direct insult, and for no reason at all. They had scarcely exchanged three words together at supper the night before, and what she had said was not terribly outrageous.

She might be a poor relation and a companion and an unmarried spinster of no particular beauty who was nearly thirty years of age and accustomed to being dismissed and ignored by gentlemen, but rarely had one bothered to be outright *rude* to her. The nerve of the man!

She took one more deep breath and began to ply her needle, doing her best to listen to the conversation behind her between Miss Hawthorne and her bosom friend, one Lady Elizabeth, or "Lizzie" to Miss Hawthorne. Spates of loud giggles interspersed with their whispers, making it almost impossible to hear anything of substance. Should she inch a little closer to hear the better?

A shadow fell over her, obstructing the warm sun through the window.

She looked up to see Mr. Parsloe standing in the precise spot that would block most of her light, gazing out at the countryside with his back to her as though he didn't have a care in the world. Her temper flared.

"Excuse me, sir!"

He swiveled and half-bent to look down at her, his collar points so high, he was unable to turn his head. A quizzing glass swung loosely from his hand.

"Ah. Miss ... Rogers, was it?"

"Rawson. You are blocking my light."

He glanced at the window, and then back at her. "I was unaware this window was exclusive for your use."

She did her best not to grind her teeth. "I

need the light for my embroidery. Kindly move out of the way, sir."

"I beg your pardon, ma'am." He sketched a bow to her and then, to her horror, sat down in the chair next to her.

Behind them, Miss Hawthorne and her friend cast a glance over their shoulders and then rose as one to promenade around the room. Grace exhaled sharply but kept her eyes on her embroidery rather than the aggravating man next to her.

"If you're going to eavesdrop, you must sit closer next time."

Grace started but kept her eyes down. She had not realized her intention had been so obvious. "I will certainly keep your advice in mind should I ever decide to eavesdrop on anyone," she said, making her voice as cold as possible.

"What are you making?"

"I do not care to converse with you. Kindly take yourself elsewhere."

"You are angry. Why?"

"Because you were rude to me."

"I was conversing with our hostess. Some might say *you* were rude for interrupting."

"And yet here you are, talking to me."

"So I am."

She finally looked up to see his considering gaze on her. His eyes were a most peculiar shade up close, a mixture of gray and green and brown that reflected the light and colors around him.

At the moment, they were also the most penetrating eyes she had ever seen, and she flushed a little beneath their regard.

"Do I have a smut on my nose?"

"No," he said. "But you do have three freckles."

Her hand flew up to cover her nose and she glared at him again. This time, it seemed to amuse him.

"I hear you are all but engaged to Sir Malcolm Stewart."

"I don't see what business it is of yours."

"I was merely curious. Is it true?"

"You will need to ask Sir Malcolm."

He continued gazing at her with those strange, unsettling eyes. "I would not advise you to accept his suit."

"Why not?"

"I don't think he would make a very good husband."

"Are you offering a better candidate?"

His laugh sounded reluctant, but genuine. "I fear not, Miss Randall."

"Rawson."

"Of course. Excuse me."

He stood up, bowed, and walked away, leaving her flushed and confused. It had been a long time since an attractive man had conversed with her. For a few moments, she had felt as though they were the only two people in the world, and her return to reality was an unpleasant bump.

Miss Hawthorne and her friend returned to their seats, casting wary glances at Grace. She ignored them. Indeed, she found it difficult to focus on their conversation. She could not stop turning the encounter with Mr. Parsloe over in her mind. The man didn't even know her. How dare he make assumptions about her personal life? Or advise her like a lecturing uncle? The arrogant cad!

Even more disconcerting was that his words echoed some of her doubts about Sir Malcolm. She was not certain the man was courting her at all, except for the fact he was an unmarried man who sought her out in conversation whenever they encountered each other in society. She had no idea if she would accept his suit or not. She felt she barely knew him even though they had been acquainted for nearly a year.

Well, there was no use worrying about it now. She bent her head to her embroidery and concentrated on trying to overhear an incriminating tidbit or two from Miss Hawthorne and her friend.

"THERE IS NOT much to tell, Aunt," Grace said with a sigh. "Miss Hawthorne is infatuated with Lord Dorchester and is plotting how to get him to dance with her at the next assembly."

"Ah, well," Harriet said philosophically. "Not every investigation yields results."

They sat in a shady spot in Lady Ashburton's garden as the sun sank in the west. It would soon be time to dress for supper, but Grace had no desire to hurry indoors, where Mr. Parsloe might lurk with more of his disconcertingly astute opinions.

Harriet looked around, breathing deeply of the scented air. "My dear Fillmore and I spent many an hour in gardens on our travels. How I miss him."

Grace reached out and grasped her aunt's hand in silent commiseration for their separate losses, and Harriet returned her squeeze before giving herself a little shake.

"Well, I don't wish to grow maudlin just

because night is approaching. Is there anyone else at the party who is, er, interesting?"

Grace frowned, feeling an odd reluctance to confide in her aunt. She finally said, "A most peculiar man. A Mr. Parsloe."

"Oh?" Harriet said.

"He's a rude and prying man. Do you know him?"

"He did not look familiar to me. Did he, er, flirt with you?"

Grace laughed despite the small sting of her aunt's words. "Aunt Harriet, you have far too much faith in my feminine attractions if you think any man would flirt with me in front of the female half of the house party."

"I think you have far too little faith in your own attractions, my dear," Harriet said. "But that's a conversation for another time. Shall we go in?"

Harriet rose to her feet, forcing Grace to rise as well. She was usually able to ignore her aunt's hints that she was too staid, too settled, but Harriet had spent her own youth gallivanting around Europe and the Americas. It was easy for her to constantly be on the lookout for her next adventure while Grace kept the household running, as she had done for her father and brother.

Not that Harriet had ever asked that of her.

Frowning, Grace followed her aunt into the house.

SEATING AT SUPPER that night was less formal, and Grace found herself next to Sir Malcolm. Over the scrape of cutlery on china, the room buzzed with the news of Napoleon's surrender to the British at the port of Rochefort, followed by his imprisonment on a British ship now headed for England.

"They are still deciding what to do with him," Lord Ashburton said, taking a sip of his wine.

"They ought to execute him," Sir Malcolm said coolly.

Grace's head turned to him in shock. "Execute a man who surrendered?"

"This is—or was—war, Miss Rawson," he said. "You suffered your own terrible loss because of Bonaparte. Don't you want to see him dead?"

Grace's hand clenched around her wineglass, and she forced herself to loosen it. "No. There's been enough death."

She looked up, anxious to avoid the direction of Sir Malcolm's conversation, and saw Mr. Parsloe's gaze on her. Those indecipherable, unexpectedly acute eyes held hers for a long moment before he looked away again to engage in lively conversation with the woman seated to his right.

Sir Malcolm noticed the direction of her gaze, and frowned. "I've been asking about that fellow," he said with a nod. "Parsloe."

"Oh?" Grace's stomach clenched, and she studied her plate rather than allow her gaze to stray back down the table to where Mr. Parsloe sat. "I hope I did not cause you any bother."

"Not at all, Miss Rawson." The frown on Sir Malcolm's face deepened. "The odd thing is, no one seems to know him. I asked Dorchester, and he denied being acquainted before now."

Grace frowned in turn. "Well, someone must know him if he was invited."

"I'm sure you're right, Miss Rawson. Still, it's most peculiar."

Grace shrugged and changed the topic to the weather, but it *was* peculiar. Most peculiar.

When she mentioned it to Aunt Harriet before bed, however, the older woman brushed the notion off. "His mother was a friend of Lady

Ashburton's. Sir Malcolm neglected to ask the ladies of the party."

"I suppose so," Grace said. "Still, it seems odd none of the gentlemen know him."

"I suspect he moves in different circles than most of the gentlemen here," Harriet said, and Grace was forced to agree.

The next morning, Mr. Parsloe was gone.

"Called back to London," Lady Ashburton said when Grace inquired. "Apparently his tailor sent word that a jacket was not coming along as he hoped, and Mr. Parsloe was forced to return." She shot a sharp look at Grace. "I didn't realize you were so interested, Miss Rawson."

"Aunt Harriet had taken an interest in him and asked me where he had gone," Grace lied smoothly. "He was, er, quite conspicuous."

"Yes, of course," Lady Ashburton said, and Grace quickly changed the topic.

If the party seemed even duller than before, Grace scolded herself out of it.

The day after that, Aunt Harriet was ready to move on. "I really can only stand a few days of conversation with the same people, and Lady

Ballinger awaits. It's only a six-hour drive from here."

"Yes, Aunt Harriet," Grace said, and went to pack her trunk.

When the topic of their departure came up in the drawing room that evening, Sir Malcolm's eyebrows rose. "By a strange coincidence, I, too, have been invited to Lady Ballinger's house party. May I offer my escort?"

"We are leaving first thing in the morning," Harriet said. "If you wish to accompany us, you certainly may."

Sir Malcolm bowed to her. "I would be honored, Mrs. Fillmore."

They made quite a procession. Sir Malcolm rode horseback beside their carriage, with his coach following behind. Parker had initially tried to insist on riding with Harriet and Grace, but Harriet consigned her to Sir Malcolm's carriage.

"You know I will want to sleep, Parker," Harriet said, "and you will be much more comfortable with Sir Malcolm's valet."

"Yes, madam," Parker said, though she and the valet eyed each other warily. There was no danger for her—she was old enough to be the young man's mother, if not his grandmother—but neither of them seemed best pleased to be stuck with the other.

Grace passed the time by staring out the window as Harriet slumbered peacefully on the other seat. Sir Malcolm would occasionally ride into her line of sight and nod at her, but she saw no point in lowering the window to converse. They would have nothing to talk about, anyway.

Again, they were the last to arrive, though getting ready for supper was not quite so much of a mad rush. Grace and Harriet were able to make a bit of an entrance to the drawing room where the rest of the guests had gathered, with Grace following a few steps behind her aunt as the older woman swept in, the plumes in her turban waving.

"Lady Ballinger!" Harriet exclaimed, and crossed to their hostess, who was getting to her feet with an air of disgruntlement.

"Ah, there you are, Mrs. Fillmore. How good to see you. And Miss Rawson with you, of course." Lady Ballinger gave Grace a curt nod and Grace bobbed a curtsey. Lady Ballinger was on the far edge of middle age, with hair an improbable shade of inky black, though Grace recalled it being a lighter brown only a few years before.

Across the room, Grace saw a figure that looked fleetingly familiar out of the corner of her eye, but when she looked again, she though she must be mistaken. The man had the unmistakable bearing of a military officer, though he was in very plain civilian dress, and sported the most magnificent side-whiskers she had ever seen, liberally sprinkled with gray. His face bore the deep tan of a man who had spent most of his life in the East—India, perhaps.

"Who is that?" she asked her hostess, who looked over with a little frown that immediately cleared.

"Ah!" she said. "That is Colonel Reynolds. He has recently returned to England from Bombay."

"I see." Grace turned away. She had an odd sensation the colonel was looking at her, but every time she looked in his direction, he was looking in a different one.

As she and her aunt moved to the group he was conversing with to be introduced, he bowed to her and Aunt Harriet a little stiffly, as though one leg was not quite as strong as the other.

Grace frowned at the colonel. "Have we met before, sir?"

"I'm certain I should remember such a meeting, Miss Rawson," he said, his voice gruff and a little hoarse. "I do not believe so."

She leaned forward a little to peer at his eyes but he turned away. It was a foolish notion, anyhow—his eyes were dark in the candlelight and Mr. Parsloe's had been that strange pale mixture of green and gray and brown she had never seen the like of before. Besides, what would Mr. Parsloe be doing at a different house party pretending to be a colonial colonel? It was mad for her to even think of it.

Still, her eyes followed him as he excused himself and walked to the other side of the room, his posture ramrod straight. It was though he were still on the parade ground despite the counterweight of his protruding belly. He limped quite noticeably, with his right leg being the weaker one. Even when standing still, she could tell he had been a military man, his arms crossed loosely behind his body in a parade rest as he tilted his head to listen to their hostess.

He still seemed strangely familiar despite his denial.

With an internal shake, Grace turned away to concentrate on the small group's conversation. No, it was absurd. The man was probably some relation of Mr. Parsloe's and that was why she detected a resemblance. Everyone her aunt knew seemed to be related to everyone else to some degree. To think otherwise would raise more questions than it answered, such as why Mr. Parsloe would decide to carry out such a masquerade and what he hoped to gain by it. She was letting her imagination run away with her.

Dismissing the colonel from her mind, she turned to Aunt Harriet, who was smiling at her.

"The colonel is a fine figure of a man, isn't he?"

Startled, Grace said, "Yes, I suppose so."

"Perhaps he will be seated next to you at supper."

Like Mr. Parsloe had been. "Perhaps."

THE COLONEL WAS NOT SEATED NEXT to Grace at supper. He was seated next to Harriet. To Grace's displeasure, the man immediately began flirting with her aunt. To her even greater displeasure, Harriet flirted back, looking more light-hearted than she had since her husband had died.

Grace sat too far away to hear their murmured words, but she could hear the peals of their laughter as she clenched her napkin into a ball. It was ridiculous they would flirt like that at their age while she was stuck with …

Her mind shied away from completing the

thought as Sir Malcolm turned to her and smiled. They were seated together again, and Grace feared arriving with him had cemented the idea of his courting her in their hostess's mind.

"Is something wrong, Miss Rawson?"

She pasted a false smile on her face. "Not at all, Sir Malcolm."

He gazed steadily at her until she wanted to shift in her chair like a schoolgirl waiting to be scolded. At last, he said, "I hope you know I would stand your friend if you should find yourself in any trouble."

She blinked, startled by the unexpected offer. "I, er, I thank you, Sir Malcolm, but I do not anticipate being in any trouble."

"Still, I hope you will keep me in mind."

"Thank you," she said, and changed the subject. The last thing she wanted was to be in Sir Malcolm's debt.

❧ 4 ❦

The next afternoon, Grace entered Harriet's room after luncheon to find Parker applying a touch of rouge to her aunt's pale cheeks even though it was still daylight.

"Are you getting ready for tonight's musicale already?" Grace jested.

Harriet laughed. "Of course not, my dear." She accepted a straw bonnet from Parker and placed it on her head, tilting it to a rakish angle before tying the ribbon under her chin. "I'm going for a walk with Colonel Reynolds."

"I'll fetch my bonnet, then," Grace said, repressing a sigh. She had hoped to spend the afternoon curled up with the latest Minerva Press novel, but if Aunt Harriet desired a walk, then that was what they must do.

"Certainly not," Harriet said. "I am far too old to require a chaperone, and you will be decidedly *de trop*." She preened in the mirror and hummed a little tune.

"Are you setting up a flirtation with the colonel, then?" Grace asked, trying to keep her tone light.

"I don't see why not. I may be widowed, but I'm not dead yet, Grace." Her eyes met Grace's in the mirror. "Don't you think him attractive?"

"Well ..." Grace temporized.

Harriet laughed and rose from her seat to accept her gloves from Parker. "Don't worry, my child." She patted Grace's cheek. "I shall be back before you know it."

And her aunt swept out of the room, leaving an open-mouthed Grace behind.

Grace turned to Parker. "Should I follow them?"

Parker turned away with a little smile. "I don't see why you should, miss. Your aunt is old enough to know what she's about, isn't she?"

Rather at a loss, Grace returned to her own room, but found herself staring at the pages of her book without absorbing any of the words. Why was she inside on a lovely day rather than walking in the gardens with a beau? It felt as though she and her aunt had switched their proper places.

Not that it mattered, she finally decided with a sniff. Aunt Harriet could flirt with whomever she pleased, even at her age.

After a long moment, Grace finally settled enough to begin to read.

THAT EVENING, Grace found herself sitting on a chair next to Sir Malcolm as they waited for the musicale to begin. She had not planned to sit with him, but there he was.

Sir Malcolm nodded to where her aunt sat next to Colonel Reynolds near the front of the room. Even as Grace watched, their heads dipped close to one another. Harriet laughed and rapped the colonel on the arm with her fan.

"I see the colonel has made a conquest."

Grace turned to look at him, so strange was his tone. "Do you know something about Colonel Reynolds I ought to know, Sir Malcolm?"

"I don't know anything about him. No one seems to know anything about the man."

Grace turned to look at the pair again, but

their hostess bustled to the front of the room to announce the first performance, and the moment was lost.

She grew more concerned as the days passed and the colonel seemed to spend every available moment of his time with Harriet. Even more frustrating was the fact Harriet refused to discuss the flirtation with Grace, who began to wonder if the man was under the impression Harriet had more money than she did.

"I see your aunt and Colonel Reynolds are together again," Sir Malcolm said to Grace as they followed the rest of the group to a picnic on the grounds near a folly the previous Lord Ballinger's father had put up when they were fashionable thirty years before. Harriet clung to the colonel's arm in a way that irritated Grace and, as usual, their heads were angled together as they flirted in whispers.

"Yes," Grace said with a frown. "They are quite inseparable."

Sir Malcolm shook his head. "I would be most cautious if I were you, Miss Rawson. It is not unheard of for … mature ladies' heads to be turned and their fortunes to be stolen."

Grace laughed, though it was more mechanical than she would have liked. "To be perfectly frank, Sir Malcolm, there is not much to steal."

"Nevertheless," he said, "I'm sure you would prefer not to do without what little you and your aunt have."

Grace felt a simultaneous desire to give Sir Malcolm the cold shoulder for his impertinence and shake her aunt until her teeth rattled. Or perhaps shake the colonel, if she could move him.

Then, the day before their planned departure for the next house party, the colonel disappeared, urgently required by his family in Yorkshire, or so their hostess said. Harriet seemed to take the news with a reassuring nonchalance, though Grace could still feel Sir Malcolm's eyes following her and Harriet as they moved through the remaining entertainments.

As she and Harriet prepared to leave the drawing room that evening, Sir Malcolm stepped into their path and bowed over Grace's hand. She returned it to her side as quickly as she decently could. Sir Malcolm's hovering was becoming rather an annoyance.

"I hope you will once again allow me to escort you, Mrs. Fillmore. The roads are too dangerous for ladies traveling alone."

"I did not realize Mrs. Carlisle had invited

you as well, Sir Malcolm," Harriet said. Her tone remained genial, but Grace could feel her aunt's slight stiffness.

"She was kind enough to extend an invitation when I expressed my interest. I only just received her note this afternoon."

Unable to resist an urge to annoy her aunt as much as her aunt had annoyed her the past few days, Grace said, "In that case, Sir Malcolm, we would be honored to accept your assistance."

Sir Malcolm bowed again, his smile a bit too smug for Grace's comfort, but allowed them to pass.

As they mounted the stairs, Harriet said in a low voice, "I do hope you are not planning to encourage Sir Malcolm, Grace."

"I don't see what business that is of yours, Aunt Harriet," Grace said, and was pleased to hear her aunt's teeth click together in irritation. In truth, she had decided to refuse Sir Malcolm's suit should he ever come up to the point, but she saw no reason to reassure Harriet when her aunt was keeping her own secrets.

❦ 5 ❦

The next morning, only Aunt Harriet's carriage stood in the drive. Grace looked around in puzzlement as Sir Malcolm strode towards them from the direction of the stables. His color was high, and he was clearly fuming from some irritation.

"I beg your pardon, ladies," he said, "but I have been informed one of the wheels of my coach has been damaged. We must wait for my coachman to fetch the carriage-maker from the village for the repair. It is, *apparently*, beyond the skills of Lord Ballinger's man. We will have to put our trip off until tomorrow."

"Impossible," Harriet said. "We are expected, and it would be quite rude of us to delay."

"At least allow me to travel with you," Sir

Malcolm said. "My coachman can follow once the repair is complete."

Harriet shook her head. "We cannot inconvenience you so, Sir Malcolm, and there is no room in the carriage since my maid will need to ride with us. I am happy to make your excuses to Mrs. Carlisle and explain you will be arriving tomorrow instead."

His frustration clear, Sir Malcolm had no choice but to bow politely. "Thank you, Mrs. Fillmore. I appreciate you doing me the courtesy."

Harriet inclined her head and allowed Lady Ballinger's footman to hand her into the carriage. Sir Malcolm caught at Grace's arm as she started to follow suit.

"Can I not persuade you to delay, Miss Rawson?"

"I am sorry, Sir Malcolm," she said, "but as my aunt's companion, I must do as she wishes."

Grace stared down at his hand until Sir Malcolm dropped her arm and stepped back. She mounted the steps into the coach and seated herself beside Parker as the carriage lurched into motion. Harriet was already settling herself for her nap in the rear-facing seat, and Parker drew some mending from the canvas bag at her feet.

"That was peculiar," Grace said.

Harriet's eyes drifted back open. "What, dear?"

"Sir Malcolm. He seemed determined to go with us."

"I told you not to encourage him," Harriet murmured, ignoring Grace's glare as she drifted off to sleep, far too conveniently for Grace to continue the argument that, in actuality, Aunt Harriet had first told *her* of Sir Malcolm's possible interest when Grace had not seen it at all.

Grace was sufficiently vexed that she composed herself for sleep as well, despite the carriage's motion seeming to jolt her back awake every time she started to nod off.

Still, she must have fallen asleep at some point, because otherwise the jolt that nearly knocked her to the floor would not have startled her so. Harriet came awake in an instant, bracing herself against the wall of the carriage to avoid being thrown from the seat. The coachman's curses pierced through wood and padding, clearly audible even before Grace opened the hatch.

"What's the trouble, Tompkins?"

"Some damn fool nearly run us off the road," Tompkins grumbled, "and now he's half in a ditch himself."

Grace parted the curtains to peer out. She had been expecting a phaeton or other light rig—the gentlemen who drove them seemed to be most careless—but instead it was a heavy, old-fashioned coach with closed curtains. The two men climbing down from the front and back of the carriage looked rather ... ominous. A chill crept along the back of her neck.

From above, Tompkins called out, "I have my musket at the ready. Move along, you."

A shot rang out, and Grace screamed without meaning to. Parker threw her to the floor, a glint of something shiny in her hand. A pistol! Where had Parker gotten a pistol?

Harriet yanked Grace to lay flat on the floor, wordlessly showing her how to protect her head as the coach swayed precariously and the coachman cursed again. Parker remained crouched by the small window, intently watching the action outside through a gap in the curtains.

Grace's heart raced out of control as she swallowed against the nausea that tickled the back of her throat. If it was highwaymen, they rarely left their victims alive. She felt a mad urge to fling open the door of the carriage and run.

"Stay *down*, miss," Parker hissed without looking. "Protect your aunt."

Even as Grace rolled towards Harriet,

another shot rang out, this one from a distance, followed by another a few seconds later. Not a musket—a rifle.

Parker chuckled and lowered her pistol, shoulders relaxing. "That's put them on the run."

Grace cautiously raised herself to her knees and peered out the window to see the ominous coach making a hasty departure, with one of the ruffians flinging himself onto the box as it drove away. From the opposite direction, a man riding towards them waved exuberantly. She lowered her window to see and hear him the better.

"I say!"

He was dressed in clerical garb, the rifle in his hand an odd contrast to the rest of his shabby genteel appearance. His legs bowed out awkwardly from too-short stirrups and a pair of tinted glasses threatened to slide down his nose.

Grace could not stop staring. The man seemed all too familiar, but she could not say precisely what made her suspicious. *Something* about him reminded her very strongly of both Mr. Parsloe and Colonel Reynolds, though he did not resemble either of them at first glance. Except perhaps in his height.

She wanted to remove his tinted glasses and check the color of his eyes.

The gentleman pulled up his horse, which sidled at the impertinence, and beamed at them, showing off large and rather stained teeth. "Lucky I was hunting nearby, eh? The highwaymen are getting bolder every day, I fear."

Harriet resumed her place on the carriage seat and lowered her own window to beam back at the man. "Your arrival was most timely, sir."

"Not at all, not at all," he said, still smiling amiably at all of them. "Only glad I could help."

"Will you … will you check on our coachman?" Grace said, trying to still the tremble in her voice. "I fear he was shot."

She was itching to get down from the carriage to see for herself, but Parker blocked the way by fussing over Harriet, who didn't seem particularly perturbed at their adventure. Grace heard some conversation outside and a groan from Tompkins before their rescuer reappeared at the window.

"The bullet only grazed him, but he's broken his arm falling off the coach. The groom will have to drive the rest of the way. I hope you're not traveling far."

"To Hillsgate," Harriet said.

Grace frowned at her aunt, trying to send a message she should not be so forthcoming with a complete stranger when they had so nearly been robbed once already, but Harriet avoided her gaze.

"Splendid!" The gentleman bowed from the saddle even as his horse tried to sidle away again. "I am the Reverend Samuel Watkins, and I have the honor of being the curate in the village there. Pray allow me to escort you the rest of the way."

"That is very good of you," Harriet said. "Thank you, sir."

There was a bit more fuss as Watkins and the groom assisted Tompkins onto the seat at the back of the coach, but after a few more minutes, Grace was able to settle into her seat as the coach began to move. Mr. Watkins put his horse into motion and trotted beside them, beaming at Grace whenever she happened to glance out the window at him. Those teeth of his were really quite odd if one looked at them too often. Almost unnatural.

Grace looked over to see that her aunt was not only awake, but watching her with surprisingly keen eyes.

"Well, that was most peculiar," Harriet said. "But no harm done."

"Yes," Grace said. "Most peculiar."

Not to mention most fortuitous the Reverend

Mr. Watkins had just happened to appear at the right time. It could be a coincidence, of course, but Grace suspected nothing that had befallen her and her aunt so far on this trip had been a coincidence. Perhaps not even her first meeting with Mr. Parsloe ... or whatever his real name might be.

❦   6   ❦

Their arrival at Hillsgate caused a bit of a stir, with Mrs. Carlisle sending for the local surgeon to set Tompkins' broken arm and insisting the Reverend Mr. Watkins stay for supper to be thanked for his heroism, but there was another shock to come.

"It is the most dreadful thing!" their hostess said. "A robbery at the Ballingers' home! Jewelry missing, and some plate as well. Everyone from the house party is being investigated."

"Not us, surely," Grace said with a laugh she did not feel.

"Everyone, my dear Miss Rawson! The note I received said a Bow Street Runner is coming here to question those of you who were at the previous party. Dreadful, simply dreadful."

Harriet was shaking her head. "I really cannot take it all in. I must rest before supper."

"Of course, of course. I will have a footman show you to your rooms." Mrs. Carlisle patted Harriet's hand. "If you need to have supper in your room, simply have your maid send word to the kitchen."

"Thank you," Harriet said, the back of her other hand pressed to her forehead as her body sagged towards Grace. "If I can possibly come down, I shall. After all, I would hate for Reverend Watkins to think his heroism was in vain."

Parker and Grace each took one of Harriet's arms and helped her up the stairs. Her aunt was quite convincingly limp against Grace's supporting hand, and she began to worry. Harriet was prone to melodrama, but the events of the day had been enough to rattle anyone's nerves.

"Now, Aunt Harriet," Grace said soothingly as they entered her aunt's room. "You know we have nothing to worry about. Everyone knows we are not thieves. Here, let me fetch your lavender water so Parker can bathe your temples."

As Parker hovered over Harriet, helping her lay down on the bed, Grace opened the traveling box that held her aunt's cosmetics and lotions. There, sitting in the middle of the bottles, was an ugly ruby brooch she had never seen before.

"What is it, dear?"

Grace grabbed the lavender water and slammed the case shut as she handed it to Parker. "Nothing, Aunt Harriet."

How dare he? *He* must have put the brooch there—no one else could or would have done it. She was more certain than ever *he* would appear at the party, if only to retrieve it. Her only question was if he would remain in his current disguise or adopt a different one.

The Bow Street Runner arrives tomorrow.

She would need to hide the brooch. Somewhere the runner wouldn't think to look. She couldn't keep it on her person—the man might think to search them. It must not be left anywhere in Aunt Harriet's room. The poor dear soul would have no way of explaining how it had gotten there. Grace had stayed in this house several times before—did she know it well enough to hide something in it?

And then she had a terrible thought.

"I'll just help Parker unpack your things, shall I?" Grace said to her aunt. If *he* had dared burden her aunt with any of his other stolen goods …

"Well, I suppose," Harriet said doubtfully. "But she probably don't need any help. Very efficient woman, you know."

Parker gave Grace an indignant look. "Thank you, miss, but I do not require any help."

"Of course not, Parker," Grace said soothingly. "But, er … I've been trying to find one of Aunt Harriet's shawls and I hope you can help me. I fear we may have left it at Lady Ashburton's."

"Certainly not, Miss Grace!" Parker said. "I always check all of madam's possessions before we leave any house."

"Even so, Parker," Grace said. "I would like to check."

Grace tried to be as thorough as possible despite the grumbling Parker hanging over her shoulder, but she didn't find anything else out of place. Just that damned brooch appearing out of nowhere, and how was she to retrieve it from her aunt's vanity case now that Parker was hovering?

"Aunt Harriet," she said, "do you still have that freckle lotion you were so kind as to purchase for me?"

Harriet brightened despite her avowed headache. "Why, yes, dear. I kept it with my cosmetics, just in case you changed your mind."

"Thank you, dear aunt." Grace bent down and kissed Harriet's cheek as Parker laid a fresh lavender-soaked handkerchief across the older woman's forehead. "I'm sorry I flew out at you as I did about it, and I appreciate your kindness."

Grace retrieved the bottle of freckle lotion, slipped the ruby brooch into her bodice, and let herself out of the room with a smile while her mind raced. Where to hide the damned brooch? Not in her own room—any Runner worth his salt would look there. And certainly not in her aunt's room. Which rooms would be unexceptionable places for her to be and yet not a place where she would be the one suspected of leaving the brooch?

It came to her in a flash. *The library, of course.* She was in and out of there all the time looking for books for her aunt. No one would be surprised to find her there, but it was also a room all of the guests had access to, so it would be difficult to pin the blame on her.

She would sneak down to the library after everyone else was in bed and hide the brooch there.

Grace slipped the brooch into the pocket of one of her pelisses when the housemaid left to take her supper dress downstairs to press it. Her panic began to subside, which allowed her suspicions to rise again. There was no way *he* could have gained admittance to Mrs. Carlisle's house party by himself. She would never admit someone with as cloudy a past as Mr. Parsloe or Colonel Reynolds had presented.

She sank onto the edge of the bed at the pieces assembled themselves in her head.

Could *he* have staged that "rescue" so he could be admitted to the party by herself and Aunt Harriet? They were unimpeachable sources who would attest to his good character thanks to his heroic actions on the road, foiling highwaymen ... who perhaps had not been highwaymen at all? She was ready to assume *he* was capable of any sort of crime to gain access to his potential victims. If jewelry and plate were missing, he could only be a common thief despite his cleverness.

She needed to protect Aunt Harriet from being accused of his crimes, no matter the cost.

WHEN THEY WENT DOWN to supper, Grace was not surprised to see the Reverend Mr. Watkins standing in a corner of the drawing room, a teacup in his hand and a benevolent smile on his face. In the darkened room, she was unable to see the color of his eyes, but he was not wearing the tinted glasses from earlier.

She felt a pang of doubt. He was so diffident, his shoulders hunched, his neck drooping like a shy bird's. What if she was wrong? If she was, she might embarrass herself in front of a roomful of people.

Taking her courage in her hands, she approached him. "Good evening, Mr. Watkins."

"Good evening, Miss ... I'm afraid we were not properly introduced this afternoon."

"No, we were not. I am Miss Rawson."

He bowed, still balancing the teacup, though it tilted precariously. "I take it neither you nor your aunt came to any harm after this afternoon's excitement."

"We are well, thank you for asking."

She leaned forward to see the color of his eyes, but the corner in which they were standing was too dark.

"Is something wrong, Miss Rawson?"

"No," she said. "It's only that you ... remind me of someone."

"I hear that often," he said. "I'm quite an ordinary-looking fellow, and people frequently mistake me for someone else."

"Of course," she said, and stepped back. *She*

could not be sure. "Well, thank you again for helping us this afternoon."

"It was my pleasure, Miss Rawson."

He bowed again; she nodded and walked away. But she could have sworn his gaze followed her.

She turned as the doors to the drawing room opened and Sir Malcolm entered the room. He immediately crossed to her, showing more emotion than she had ever seen him evince before. He tried to grasp her hand, but she pulled it out of reach to toy with her fan instead.

"My dear Miss Rawson! I have just been told of your and your aunt's misadventure this afternoon. If only I had been with you as I had wished."

"It was not your fault, Sir Malcolm," she said, wishing he would leave her alone so she would have a moment to think. "No one can control where and when highwaymen will strike."

"Still, I feel responsible. You and your aunt are lucky nothing worse happened."

"Yes," Grace said. "We are."

The butler announced supper, and all of the guests filed in, still buzzing about the events of the day.

Grace watched Reverend Watkins at supper

as best she could, still unsure if it was really *him*. Could this be the third disguise she had seen him in? And could he be the thief the Runner sought? She wanted to deny it, but the sinking of her stomach let her know it was the most logical conclusion.

It was just her luck she would become fascinated by a common thief.

She felt Sir Malcolm watching her from the other end of the table, so she flashed him a smile before she turned to the supper partner on her other side to make conversation about the weather. Sir Malcolm did not smile back, and seemed to be watching her in a way that made her skin prickle unpleasantly. Surely he wasn't jealous? He hadn't seemed to be sufficiently attached to her for that kind of emotion, but perhaps the afternoon's events and his chagrin at not being there to help her and Aunt Harriet had heightened his emotions. She certainly hoped not.

Reverend Watkins slipped away sometime between the end of supper and when the gentlemen re-joined the ladies. Grace was both relieved and disappointed. She spent the rest of the evening in desultory conversation while she waited on pins and needles to have time and privacy to hide the brooch.

7

G race allowed a housemaid to help her into her nightdress and braid her hair for the night before dismissing her. Once alone, she paced her room. She didn't want to take the risk of falling asleep. If the twice-damned brooch was still in her possession once the Runner arrived …

Visions of herself in the dock at the Old Bailey kept her fully awake until the sounds of the house quietened down for the evening. She slipped into her pelisse and listened at her bedroom door for a long moment until she was sure all sounds of movement outside had ceased.

Carefully, she cracked the door open and slipped into the hallway, candle in hand. She only had to conceal herself once on the way to the library, but the near-miss sent her heart pounding and she could not steady her breathing until she reached the door of the library and stepped inside, closing it behind her as quietly as she could.

The brooch seemed to burn a hole in her pocket as she set the candle on a table and turned a slow circuit. Where was the best place to conceal the thing? Would she implicate her host by hiding it in his desk? It might be better to tuck it onto a bookshelf to be discovered later.

Her breath caught as a deeper shadow separated itself from a corner and moved towards her. It formed itself into the figure of a man and, as he stepped into the circle of light cast by her candle, she knew him. He was still dressed as Reverend Watkins ... but now she knew for certain it had been *him* all along, Mr. Parsloe and Colonel Reynolds and Reverend Watkins. His entire demeanor had changed, and it was as though a completely different man stood inside the same clothes. He smiled at her, and she saw he had discarded the false teeth.

"Good evening, Miss Rawson," he murmured. "Fancy meeting you here."

"What are *you* doing here?" she hissed, trying to keep her voice as low as his.

"Just having a look around."

"Looking for a few things to steal?"

"I don't know what you mean, Miss Rawson."

A small smile played across his mobile lips, and she looked away, unnerved to find herself fascinated with a man's mouth. And the rest of him. He stood tall and straight now, no longer the shy curate. His shoulders were wider than she remembered, even without the extra padding he had worn as Mr. Parsloe.

She was far too acutely aware the only thing she wore beneath her respectable pelisse was a thin lawn nightrail.

She was tempted to accuse him of putting the brooch in her aunt's cosmetics case and have it out with him immediately, but she bit her tongue. What did she know of this man, after all? Her words could hang him, and he might decide to silence her if she confronted him with what she suspected. Until she knew how he would react, it might be better to keep her own counsel and hide the brooch once he left the room.

"The Bow Street Runner will be here tomorrow," she whispered.

"Ah. Then it is a good thing I will not be."

"I can send him to wait on you at the rectory."

"Alas, he will not find me there." He fixed those odd gray-green eyes on her. "But you already knew that, I think."

She took a step backwards, feeling a buzz of danger in the too-close space between her and the mesmerizing power of those eyes. "What am I to call you?"

"What do you want to call me?"

Grace bit her tongue and glared at him.

He laughed softly. "No need to be profane, my dear girl. You don't want to shock me."

"Trouble. I call you Trouble."

He bowed slightly in acceptance of the name, the mocking smile still playing on his lips. "You ought to be more careful, skulking around other people's houses in the middle of the night. You never know who you might run into."

"Careful about what?" Grace let out a harsh, unamused laugh, then bit her lip as it seemed to echo in the quiet room. She lowered her voice again. "Being alone with a man? Believe me, sir, I have learned through long experience that men are very able to control themselves around an aging spinster like me."

"And yet I doubt Sir Malcolm has seen you like this."

He looked her up and down in a lazy way that made her pull the pelisse tighter at her throat. She could swear his piercing eyes saw right through the fabric to the thin nightdress beneath—and even further.

"If he had," he said, "the man might have come up to the mark by now."

A flush raced across her face of equal parts embarrassment and anger … and perhaps something more. "That's no way for a clergyman to talk."

His smile held a sharp edge of cynicism. "Come, come, my dear. There's no need for dissembling between us. You know very well I'm no clergyman."

With the slow grace of a tiger, he began pacing towards her.

She backed away, an impulsive action of survival. When she stumbled over a low table, he sprang forward and pulled her against him, trapping her arms at her sides.

"Unhand me, sir!" Grace snapped, hoping her voice did not sound as shaky as she feared. His body was warm and hard, and she felt a strange urge to let herself sink against him. She supposed it was because her knees had turned to water and were refusing to support her.

"Not just yet," he said, his voice oddly

thoughtful. One of his hands went down to loosely hold her wrists behind her back while the other came up to cradle her jaw.

"This is a very bad idea," Grace croaked out as his head dipped towards her.

"I know." He sounded almost apologetic before his lips came down on hers.

Grace was not completely inexperienced. She had had her season in Bath, and had exchanged a few kisses with a swain or two in the gardens of the local squire's house when they had taken an evening stroll.

Now she realized they had all been clumsy boys.

This was a man. A man who knew what he wanted and how to coax her into giving it. His grasp on her wrists loosened but, rather than pushing him away, her arms crept around his neck of their own volition, pulling him closer and freeing his hands to cup her backside and pull her against him with a sudden fierceness before she was abruptly freed, bereft in the middle of the room.

She swayed towards him, but he took a step back out of the circle of her candle's light. She could almost see him pull the cloak of cynicism back around himself.

"Behave yourself, Grace," he said, and vanished through the open French doors.

She stared after him, still dazed, until some instinct warned her to check the pocket of her pelisse.

The brooch was gone.

8

The next morning, Grace was on her way back to her room after a morning walk to try and calm the fury that had kept her up half the night when her aunt's door opened and Parker's head popped out.

"Miss, I'll need you in here at once. Your aunt is feeling poorly."

"Oh, dear." Grace quickened her steps to find her aunt still lying in bed, her face pale and her gray-streaked braid tumbled over her shoulder. She smiled weakly at Grace and put a hand out.

"So foolish of me," she said. "I must have eaten something at supper that disagreed with me."

Grace crossed the room to take her aunt's hand, trying to calm herself. Harriet's hand was a little clammy, but her grip was strong. "I'll ring for some warm broth."

Harriet made a face. "If you insist, my dear, but I cannot promise I will be able to keep it down."

As Grace crossed to the bellpull, a commotion in the hallway caused her to pause. She and Parker looked at each other before Parker moved to the door. She opened the door at the same moment a peremptory rap thundered on it.

A tall, gaunt man dressed in the dark blue coat and red waistcoat of a Bow Street Runner stood in the doorway, frowning ferociously at all of them. Harriet shrank back against the pillows with a faint cry, and Parker placed herself between the angry Runner and her mistress.

"And who might you be, my good man?" Parker said. "Can't you see my mistress is not well? Take yourself off!"

The man gave her an inimical glare and said, "I have permission from Mr. Carlisle to search the rooms. All of the rooms."

"It's all right, Parker," Harriet said in a weak voice. "You must let the man do his job."

"Right," the man said.

Grace stepped in front of him, forcing him to halt a second time.

"What is your name, sir?"

He looked down at her, his features sharp and impassive. After a long moment, one corner of his mouth quirked, and he said, "Smith."

"Well, Mr. Smith, my aunt has given her permission for your search, but you must work as quickly and as quietly as you can."

Smith grunted, which Grace supposed was all the acknowledgement she was going to receive. She retreated back to her aunt's bedside, standing shoulder-to-shoulder with Parker.

Another man in the same clothing came in and they began rummaging through everything in the room, checking every drawer, every shelf, every container and trunk belonging to her aunt. They went into Harriet's dressing room, and Parker followed to keep an eye on them.

Harriet gestured to Grace to come closer, and Grace leaned in.

Harriet murmured, "I wish you'd told me earlier you'd removed it, my dear. I wouldn't have had to go to all of this trouble."

Grace jerked back and stared at her aunt, who had a rueful smile on her face. Harriet couldn't mean she had known the brooch was in her luggage!

The two Runners came back into the room, their scowls showing they had found nothing.

The one called Smith glared at Harriet and then smiled in a most sinister manner.

"We must search the bed as well."

"Sir!" Grace said, her fear adding more force to the shock in her voice. "My aunt is a lady and should not be pestered this way."

"We represent the law, miss, and we will do what is necessary," Smith retorted. "Get her out of that bed."

Parker ordered them to turn their backs as she and Grace helped Harriet into an enveloping dressing gown. They led Harriet to sit in the lone armchair in the room, where she leaned her head against the cushions with her eyes closed.

The two men stripped the bed down to the mattress and searched every possible crevice. Again, they found nothing. Smith's face had become a frozen mask of rage as the futile search dragged on, and his eyes blazed with cold fury as he came to stand in front of Harriet.

"Where is the brooch?" he hissed, and Grace flinched.

Harriet leaned forward and vomited on his boots.

"I'M QUITE ALL RIGHT NOW," Harriet murmured. "It was just a little salt water."

It had been a chaotic scene after Harriet vomited on Smith's boots, with Smith spitting curses that caused Grace to cover her ears before he stormed out, leaving Mrs. Carlisle to stand in the doorway wringing her hands. Grace had been able to hand a—thankfully empty— chamber pot to Parker so Harriet could purge her stomach one more time before Grace and Parker helped her into the re-made bed.

Grace insisted Parker take herself off to the kitchen for a cup of tea once the housemaid had cleaned up the mess on the floor and Harriet was settled.

Now she and her aunt were alone in the room with the curtains drawn against the sun. Harriet rested against the pillows with her eyes closed, her face drawn and pale.

"What did you say, Aunt Harriet?"

Harriet opened her eyes. She looked tired, but her gaze was clear. "Salt water. It works like a charm when you need to make yourself sick in a hurry."

Grace rubbed her forehead. "And why did you need to make yourself sick?"

"To prevent them from finding the brooch, of course." She smiled sunnily at Grace. "I didn't realize you had already taken care of it, you clever girl."

"Why did you have it?"

Harriet cocked her head and looked at Grace, but a swift knock on the door made her close her mouth again as their hostess bustled in.

"I hope you are feeling better, Mrs. Fillmore?" Mrs. Carlisle asked in a quavering voice.

Harriet's eyes drooped and she leaned back against the pillows, the picture of delicate, ladylike illness. "Much better. I'm sorry to be so foolish. It must have been something I ate."

Mrs. Carlisle's hands twisted together. "Oh, dear. Oh, dear. None of the other guests seem to have been ill."

"My aunt has quite a delicate stomach," Grace said, a little surprised at how easily the lie came to her. "Some foods make her ill that never bother anyone else. Isn't that right, Auntie?"

"Quite right," Harriet said, her voice a little stronger.

Mrs. Carlisle straightened, a hopeful look on her face. "As long as it's not the cholera. I do dread the cholera."

"I feel I can assure you it's not cholera," Grace said, somehow keeping a straight face, and Mrs. Carlisle sighed.

"I think some broth will set me quite right," Harriet said.

Their hostess brightened. "But of course! I should have thought of that sooner. I'll have a maid bring some right away."

Then Parker came back into the room and shooed Grace out. She stood irresolute in the hallway for a long moment before walking to her own room.

It had been torn apart.

She stood staring in the doorway, stunned by the wreckage. Every piece of clothing she owned had been taken out of the wardrobe and flung to the floor. Half the drawers were still open. The bed was stripped down to the mattress, which lay askew, as though they had pulled it up and not placed it back correctly. Boot prints covered her undergarments, her dresses, the blankets, everything that was on the floor.

"Oh, Miss!"

Grace turned to see an aghast maid behind her, her arms full of linens. "Oh, Miss, what have they done to your room?"

Grace tried to shrug, but the sick anger at the pit of her stomach stopped the movement. They had done this in revenge, of course, because she had defied them in Harriet's room.

"They were looking for some missing jewelry, but I do not have it."

The maid stared still. "Let me go fetch Mary and a footman or two and we'll have this set to rights in no time."

Grace crossed to the dressing room, picking up garments as she went so she would not step on them, and peered inside. It was just as much of a mess as the bedroom, and she felt a surge of fury at the men who had done this, who had violated her belongings this way.

Her anger spread out to the man who had caused this by saddling her aunt with the ruby brooch in the first place and then disappeared with it at the first sign of trouble.

That was all he was to her. Trouble. No matter how well he kissed.

9

"I think we will need to move on to Lady Ridley's party sooner rather than later," Aunt Harriet murmured later that evening as they waited in the drawing room to go in to supper.

Grace couldn't help but agree. They found themselves in isolation at one end of the room, the rest of the guests eying them suspiciously and murmuring to each other. The rampage and shouts of the Bow Street Runners—who had left in a huff after searching Grace's room—could not be concealed from the other guests, and even their hostess now regarded Grace and Harriet with an edge of doubt.

The only person who seemed willing to speak to them was the last person Grace wanted to speak to: Sir Malcolm. He approached them as soon as he entered the room and bowed to Harriet and Grace in turn.

"Miss Rawson. Mrs. Fillmore. I am so sorry you were troubled."

Grace inclined her head. "Thank you, sir." Then, when he remained standing, she repressed a sigh and said, "Will you have a seat?"

"Thank you." He sat beside her. "What were they searching for?"

"I don't entirely remember."

Aunt Harriet fanned herself, leaning back. She was still a bit pale after her illness of that afternoon, and Sir Malcolm eyed her nervously. He must have heard what had happened to Smith's boots.

"I think they said something about jewelry," Grace said. "But of course they found nothing."

Sir Malcolm clicked his tongue. "Dreadful. And you know nothing about a missing brooch?"

Grace met his eyes steadily, not wavering for a moment. "Nothing."

She couldn't help but wonder how Sir Malcolm had known it was a missing brooch the Runners had been searching for.

Aunt Harriet announced at the conclusion of supper that her dear friend Lady Ridley had asked her to come early, and everyone nodded politely and murmured about how she would be missed. Both of Grace's supper partners had spoken only the bare minimum to her, and Sir Malcolm watched her with a sharpness she no longer mistook for infatuation. He was watching both her and Harriet, and likely had been since the beginning of their trip.

That night as Grace was finishing her braid, Parker came to tap on her door.

"Madam would like you to sleep in her room tonight."

"Is she feeling ill again?" Grace asked anxiously.

Parker shook her head. "She is feeling nervous and would prefer you sleep in her room tonight."

"All right." Grace threw her pelisse over her nightdress and followed Parker back to her aunt's room.

Harriet was already tucked up, but she smiled at Grace. "Thank you, my dear. After our, er, visitors this afternoon, I kept picturing them knocking at our doors again and I could not sleep."

"I'm sure no one would bother you, Aunt Harriet," Grace said as Parker turned down the covers on the opposite side of the bed. It was an old Tudor bed with room for at least four adults, though it appeared Parker would be taking herself back to her cot in the dressing room rather than joining them.

"It was not for myself I was worried, Grace," her aunt said, before pinching out the candle and rolling over.

Grace resisted an urge to grind her teeth in frustration. Why must Aunt Harriet be so mysterious about the strange goings-on? Whatever her aunt was hiding from her, it was clearly something Grace needed to know, whether she wanted to or not.

She turned her own back to her aunt and settled herself for sleep. She had to admit that she did feel a bit better knowing that Harriet and Parker were nearby. If she had stayed in her room alone, she would have been listening for footsteps at her door all night.

WHEN HER AUNT announced with unusual morning vigor at the crack of dawn that they would be leaving for Devon as soon as they could pack, Grace kept her inward groan to herself. She was not looking forward to another day of being jounced around by the carriage, but it was better than continuing to be shunned by the rest of the guests.

There was nothing more for her to worry about, she reassured herself as she returned to her own room. *He* would not dare show his face to her again—not after what he had done. He was likely already miles away with his stolen goods, laughing up his sleeve at her and her aunt after their experience with the Bow Street Runners.

She opened her vanity case and her sigh cracked into a shriek as she jerked her hand away from it.

The ruby brooch glinted in the morning sun from its place on top of her hairbrush.

She stared at it for a long moment, almost unwilling to believe her eyes. *Impossible.* It could not … perhaps she was going mad. Yes, that made more sense than to think the damned brooch had re-appeared in her baggage like a malicious magician's trick.

But its reappearance only crystallized a suspicion that had been growing since this game had first begun.

She crossed to the door of her room and locked it before picking up the brooch to examine it more closely. It was an ugly thing, though the stones were large enough to make it valuable. It was in the Egyptian style that had been so popular a decade before, with a cobra curved around the central stone, guarding it with unwinking eyes of emerald.

The catch was almost indiscernible on the back of the piece, half-hidden behind a scroll of gold on the left-hand side. She pressed it with her fingernail, and the back opened to reveal a tightly folded piece of paper.

When she unfolded it, she was no more enlightened than before—the words were gibberish, and there were numbers mixed in at seemingly haphazard intervals.

A cold chill crept up her spine as she realized what it must be: a coded message.

He wasn't a thief at all, despite what he had allowed her to believe.

He was a spy.

But for which side?

She sank down on the edge of the bed, still holding the coded message in one hand and the brooch in the other, unable to decide whether she should put the message back into its hiding place or keep it with her. There was no one she could trust with this matter. Aunt Harriet would surely dissolve into hysterics, and Parker would be no more help. The Runner's desperate search for the brooch seemed more suspicious than ever, as did Sir Malcolm's knowledge of it.

The decision made, she crossed to the small writing desk and lay the cipher down to make a copy. It seemed expedient to return the paper to its hiding place in case the brooch was discovered, but it would be prudent to preserve the information in the message itself as a safeguard.

As she copied, the question at the back of her mind still pounded at her: which side was *he* working for?

The copied cipher seemed too dangerous to keep anywhere but on her person, so she folded it into a tiny square and tucked it down into the busk pocket of her loosened stays, sliding the busk back in to cover it. Even the most thorough search would not find it there. She then replaced the original cipher back into the brooch and closed the back, hoping there was no way the next person would be able to figure out she had looked at it, or had even found it.

And now she realized she had a different problem. *He* might have been willing to abandon a piece of jewelry if he had been a mere thief, but a spy would never abandon a cipher, no matter which side he worked for. He would be back for it.

She hated herself for the little leap her heart gave at the notion. But she could not stop herself from hoping *he* was on the right side.

10

Lady Ridley's home was close to the village of Diptford in Devon, which contained a fine medieval church with a stone spire and not much else.

At least Sir Malcolm had not insisted on trying to escort them again. Grace hoped it was the scandal of having herself and Aunt Harriet searched by Bow Street Runners that had discouraged his attentions and not that he was forming another kind of plot. She could not help but notice that Sir Malcolm had appeared at the same house parties *he* had, even when it seemed Sir Malcolm had gone to quite a bit of trouble, and even changed his own plans to be there. She hoped it was not her instinctive distaste for the man that made her suspicious of him.

Lady Ridley's house was old and not in

good repair, but it boasted a beautiful view of the countryside, especially from the drawing room. As their hostess ushered them around the room, meeting and greeting the other guests, Grace scrutinized them as best she could without seeming to. To her disappointment, none of them were *him*. She felt sure by now he would not be able to conceal himself from her. They had met too many times before.

Aunt Harriet looked across the vista outside the windows and sighed with contentment. "You do have a lovely house, Lady Ridley."

"It's quite convenient, too," their hostess agreed, "what with being less than twenty miles to Plymouth. The shopping there is nearly as good as London, and the fish is always as fresh as can be."

Aunt Harriet drew close to their hostess. "Is it true you can see ... *him* in the harbor?"

"Well, not very well," their hostess said. "He shows himself on the deck several times a day, but they have anchored the ship away from any other ships, and even the smallest boats are required to keep their distance."

"Who is in the harbor?" Grace asked, and both of the older women gave her a scornful look.

"Bonaparte, of course," their hostess said. "Don't you read the newspapers?"

"Of course," Grace said. *Of course!*

Now she knew it was only a matter of time before she saw *him* again.

She was even more certain when a late-arriving guest was admitted to the drawing room after supper to make his apologies to their hostess.

"How nice to see you again, Sir Malcolm," Grace said, and extended her hand to him. She was pleased to see it did not tremble.

Sir Malcolm bowed over her hand. "A pleasure, Miss Rawson," he said, and smiled.

GRACE HAD FINISHED BRAIDING her hair for the night when she heard the soft thump outside her door. Her heart suddenly racing, she picked up her candle and crossed to the door, flinging it open as abruptly as she could.

A footman slouched against the doorframe, clutching one arm. When his strangely colored eyes met hers, she knew *he* was in trouble.

"Come in before you get blood on the carpet," she hissed, and threw the door wider.

He staggered inside and sat down on the edge of the bed, more abruptly than Grace thought he meant to. She re-locked the door before crossing to the small wardrobe and pulling out one of her petticoats to begin tearing it into strips.

"I shouldn't have come here," he said quietly.

"No," she said, "you shouldn't have." She crossed to the bed with the cloth strips in her hand and tugged on the sleeve of his jacket. Her hand came away crimson with blood.

"It's only a matter of time before they find me."

"I know," she said. "Hurry."

She finished tugging off his jacket and waistcoat and pulled his shirt over his head despite his muttered protests.

It was a bullet wound, a long gouge across his upper arm. The bleeding had slowed, but she took a deep breath anyway.

"Don't faint on me now, for God's sake!" He kept his voice barely above a murmur, but the admonishment still shot through her and stiffened her knees as she dipped the cloth into the water.

She glared at him as she sponged the worst of the blood away, then made a pad of the fabric and pressed it hard against the wound. He flinched and inhaled with a hiss, but she kept pressing until she felt confident the bleeding had stopped.

"I think it only grazed you. I didn't see a hole."

She began wrapping her makeshift bandage around his arm, her hands moving faster as her heart kicked up its pace. A half-naked man sat only inches away from her. In her bedchamber. *On her bed*.

As she had suspected, he wasn't bulky at all, but lithe as a panther stalking its prey, muscles rippling beneath his skin as he sighed. An intriguing fuzz of dark hair scattered across his chest and arrowed down towards his bloodstained breeches. Unnerved, she pulled the bandage tight and knotted it. She ought not to be … be *lusting* after an injured man.

Her doorknob rattled, and she gasped. Without a sound, he slipped under the bed, gesturing imperatively, and she shoved the washbasin under the bed along with his bloodstained coat and shirt and the remains of her petticoat.

She looked around frantically, feeling as though anyone who came in would know what was happening. She dried her hands on her nightrail as a knock sounded on the door.

"Open up!"

She took a deep breath. "Who's there?"

There was a silence beyond the door, and then another peremptory knock. "Open the door!"

Instead, she yanked at the bellpull and began to scream. "Help! Oh, help! Aunt Harriet! Lord Ridley! Help!"

She didn't stop screaming until more footsteps thundered down the hallway and a mutter of voices outside the door let her know witnesses had arrived. Snatching up her nightcap, she tied it askew on her head and put on her pelisse to cover the faint shadow of blood on her nightrail.

After some muttered discussion, a soft tap was followed by the voice of her puzzled host. "Miss Rawson? What has happened?"

She crossed to the door and unlocked it. Half the house party stood in the hallway in varying states of undress, with yawning, half-dressed servants behind them. She had no way of knowing for certain which one of them—if any—had been trying to get her to open the door, but she could see Sir Malcolm standing fully dressed at the edge of the crowd.

"Oh, Lord Ridley!" she gasped, clutching the pelisse to her throat in a dramatic grasp. "The most dreadful thing! A man was pounding on my door and demanding to be let in!"

Ridley's majestic brows drew together. "That's absurd, my dear. Nothing like that has ever happened at one of my house parties. Perhaps he, er, mistook the room?"

Grace judged the moment had come for her to weep, so she did, as the men stood around helplessly and the ladies clucked. Glancing around the crowd from under her eyelashes, she noticed that her aunt was not among those present.

Most interesting.

"Perhaps he thought someone had gone into your room," Sir Malcolm said.

She gasped. "I beg your pardon!" she said in her most freezing tones.

Everyone else turned to look at Sir Malcolm.

He flushed. "That is ... I mean to say ..."

Grace drew herself to her full height. "I resent the implication, sir." She straightened the frilly nightcap on her head and pulled her pelisse more tightly around her. She arranged her expression into the most spinsterish, vinegary one possible and knew she had succeeded when the men all subtly recoiled from her.

All except Sir Malcolm.

Quite interesting.

"Now, now, Miss Rawson," Lord Ridley said in his most condescending tone. "No one could possibly think you would do such a thing."

He turned a fulminating eye to Sir Malcolm, who looked away and said, "Of course not. My apologies, Miss Rawson."

"Very well." She sniffed. "Lord Ridley, would you be so kind as to send my aunt's maid to me? I do not feel comfortable being alone for the rest of the night."

"Certainly, Miss Rawson, certainly."

"Then I shall await her arrival. Good night."

With a decisive click, she closed the door, turned the key in the lock, and hurried over to the bed. He was already sliding out from underneath, a wry grin on his face.

"I commend you, Miss Rawson," he murmured. "You were born to be on the stage."

In a rush, Grace realized again that she was standing in her bedroom with a shirtless man while she wore only in her nightrail and pelisse. She blushed at the impropriety and tried to keep her voice as low as his.

"Has the bleeding stopped?"

"Yes, thank you." He pulled the remains of his shirt over his head, threw on his coat and waistcoat, straightened the footman's wig that sat crooked on his head, and crossed to the window.

"You can't go out that way!"

He quirked a brow at her. "I can't go through the hallway. Our, er, friend is waiting for me there."

She wrung her hands before dropping them at her sides. "Where will you go?"

"Up and over the roof, and then drop down."

"With only one arm?"

"I'll manage." His grin flashed in the darkened room. "I always do."

"Oh, very well. Break your neck if you want to."

He crossed back to her and took hold of her hand. Was he ... would he dare to ...

With another rakish grin, he kissed her palm. Her fingers curled around his without her conscious volition.

"Thank you, and good night," he said. "Hide the bloody rags under the mattress until Parker gets here."

Before she could ask how he knew Parker's name, he crossed to the window, pulled himself up and out, and vanished into the night.

A moment later, a sharp knock on the door made Grace flinch before a familiar voice said, "It's Parker, miss."

"Oh." Grace opened the door and Parker strode in, her nightcap perfectly in place despite the lateness of the hour and not a hair gone amiss from her braid. She turned, shut the door, and turned the key in the lock.

"First thing we must do," Parker said in a low voice, "is burn the evidence. Build the fire back up."

Grace gaped at her.

Parker gave her a little shove. "Hurry, now."

As Parker poured the bloody water into the chamber pot and rinsed the bowl, Grace poked at the fire until the flames were high enough to burn the still-damp remains of her petticoat. She tossed them on and watched the flames lick at them. Parker moved to her side, seeming to be equally mesmerized.

"How does he know you?" Grace said quietly as they watched the evidence burn down to smoldering ashes.

"You need to talk to Madam," Parker said. "She wants to walk with you tomorrow. Early."

11

The weather the next day was beautiful —sunny and warm, with the slightest breeze playing over the garden that overlooked the rolling countryside as Grace and Harriet strolled side by side.

Grace didn't care about any of that, and fixed her aunt with a steely gaze. Aunt Harriet was going to tell her the truth if Grace had to shake it out of her syllable by syllable.

"I *am* sorry, my dear," Aunt Harriet said. "You are quite right to be angry with me. I ought to have taken you into my confidence before we even began this trip, but I wasn't sure if you would be up to it." She beamed at Grace. "I should have known you would be."

Grace looked around as discreetly as she

could and saw no one nearby. "How long have you been a spy?"

Harriet chuckled. "Oh, well done, my dear girl. Let's see—since shortly after I married your Uncle Fillmore."

Grace stumbled to a stop and stared. "Surely Uncle Fillmore knew you were a spy."

"Of course he knew," Aunt Harriet said calmly, and nudged Grace back into motion. "You can hardly suppose I would take on such an enterprise without my husband's knowledge and permission. It would not have been at all proper to do so otherwise."

"Of course not," Grace said, her head spinning as she looked at her placid aunt. "One must be proper."

"And of course your uncle was my partner in espionage," Aunt Harriet said brightly.

"Of course he was." Grace sat abruptly on a nearby bench. Harriet took the seat next to her, looking just as placid and respectable as ever.

Her aunt must be mad, of course, insane to be making such claims, but ….

But so much about her aunt and uncle made sense now. Grace felt her world tilting on its axis, turning right side up for the first time. Their travels back and forth to the continent, even when it was closed to others. Their years in America, conveniently during the time of their revolution. Her uncle's mysterious death on the Continent, and her aunt's wordless grief. Of course Harriet couldn't discuss the circumstances. Not if he had been killed while spying.

"We are fortunate our opponent has consistently overlooked my actions," Harriet continued. "He still thinks I have merely been taking orders. Men are prone to such oversights."

"And they think you have been taking orders from …" Grace said slowly.

Harriet smiled at her again. "You know who. He has been quite frustrated with you, but in an, er, intrigued way. Just as I had hoped."

Grace wished to pursue that question, but Sir Malcolm was approaching them.

A pistol glinted in his hand.

"Good afternoon, ladies," he said. "I will join you, shall I?"

"You are not welcome, Sir Malcolm," Harriet said coolly, and Sir Malcolm laughed.

"I did not expect I would be but, as you know, one does what one must in these circumstances."

"I thought you hated Bonaparte," Grace

said, hoping to distract him. "You said he ought to be executed."

"He ought to, by rights," Sir Malcolm said with a shrug. "But his friends still pay well."

He leveled the gun at Harriet. "Now, Miss Rawson. Give me the brooch, or I shall shoot your aunt."

"Don't do it, Grace," Harriet said. "He'll shoot us both once you do."

"My dear Mrs. Fillmore, you wound me. Besides, I need both of you alive. For the moment, anyway."

"Why do you think I have it?" Grace said, praying one of the other guests would decide to go for a stroll, but the view to the house remained empty.

"I know you have it, Miss Rawson. And I know you have it on your person, because we have already searched your room."

Harriet turned a reproachful gaze on Grace, who shrugged and said, "I didn't think it was safe to leave it in my room."

"Foolish, my dear, very foolish. But I blame myself for not giving you the proper instructions."

"Yes, you ought to have," Grace said, the irritation in her voice not all feigned.

"Enough!" Sir Malcolm said. He looked

nervously towards the house and gestured with the gun. "Walk, if you please."

Silently, Grace obeyed, her aunt clinging to her arm.

Sir Malcolm guided them out of the garden and into the stand of trees across a nearby meadow. Grace glanced from side to side as they walked a narrow path, but the trees and underbrush were too thick to allow her to dart away.

They stumbled into a clearing that held a tumbledown cottage—a gamekeeper's cottage, or so Grace assumed, but not one currently in use. A wider road opened up behind it, with a horse and gig tied up to one side. As they entered the clearing, the horse looked up, its mouth still full of grass as it contemplated them and then went down for another bite. Grace suppressed the giggle that tried to bubble up in her throat at the unexpected sight, aware that her amusement held an edge of hysteria.

Sir Malcolm unlocked the door with a rusted key and stepped back, gesturing for her to open the door. It was a wretched hovel inside, with holes in the thatched roof and only a battered wooden bench for furniture.

"Sit down, Miss Rawson." He grasped

Harriet's elbow as she moved to follow Grace. "No, not you, Mrs. Fillmore. You stay with me."

Grace sank down on the bench, which was close to the trash-littered fireplace. The room was dark, with boarded-up windows that only allowed a few bits of light through. Most of the light came through the open front door.

"The brooch, Miss Rawson. Now."

She looked to Harriet, who nodded, her face resigned. Grace reached beneath her skirts and unfastened it from her petticoat. She made a gesture as if to throw it to Sir Malcolm, but the gun came up and stayed steady on her.

"No tricks, Miss Rawson. Mrs. Fillmore, kindly retrieve the brooch from your niece."

Grace handed it over, trying to read her aunt's expression, but the room was too dark.

"Very good, Miss Rawson." Sir Malcolm grasped Harriet roughly by the arm as she returned to him with the brooch, pointing the gun at her side. "I'm afraid I must take your aunt with me to ensure your friend cannot act against me, but you should be safely out of the way here."

Grace watched helplessly as Sir Malcolm backed out of the room, still holding Harriet's arm. She didn't dare make a move towards them lest he decide to shoot Harriet and take Grace as his hostage instead.

"Goodbye, Miss Rawson," Sir Malcolm said, and shut the door. The key ground in the lock, and Grace knew she was a prisoner. As she heard the clatter of the gig departing, she gulped back the tears of helplessness that threatened to overwhelm her.

Instead, she rose from the bench and groped in the dark as best she could. She shoved at the boards that closed off the windows, but they held tight, and the door was too sturdy for her to budge even when she hammered on it until she was exhausted. She *must* get out. She needed to help Aunt Harriet.

At last, she sank back down on the bench, shoulders heaving as useless tears tried to overtake her. Surely someone would come to her rescue and not leave her forgotten here.

It may have been a few minutes, or it may have been an hour, when a hard fist hammered on the door, startling her out of her haze.

"Grace?"

"Yes! Yes, I'm in here."

She took two steps towards the door before it shivered from a hard kick. Two more blows and it sprang open. *He* stood in the doorway.

"Grace," he said. "Are you all right?"

His arms were around her in a hard, comforting embrace almost before she realized she had run to him. She let herself rest against him for a long moment before she took a resolute breath and stepped back without breaking his hold on her. He was dressed in the rough clothes of an outdoor servant, but it was unmistakably *him*.

"It was Sir Malcolm. He has the brooch … and Aunt Harriet."

"Damn!" He dropped his arms from around her and looked as though he would like to hit someone, preferably Sir Malcolm.

"We haven't a chance in hell of catching up with them, but we need to try," he said. "If only we knew where they were going!"

"I have a copy of the cipher," Grace said.

"What?" He wheeled around to look at her, and she took a step back, speared by the intensity of his gaze.

"I … I made a copy. But it's …"

"Is it at the house?" he asked with barely leashed impatience.

"I hid it in my … stays."

A spark of humor—and something else—lit his strange gray-green eyes. "The ones you're wearing, I hope."

"I only have the … that is … yes."

She stood awkwardly for a long moment before understanding dawned for him.

"Grace. Do you need me to unlace your stays?"

Her throat was so suffused with embarrassment she couldn't speak, only nod.

"Well, it's the first time I've used that excuse," he murmured, and stepped closer to her. With a gasp, she backed a few steps away.

"I don't have to ... to ... I only need to loosen them so I can get the paper out. But I can't do it by myself." She undid the buttons of her spencer and removed it. He grinned as he took the garment from her and draped it over his forearm like a valet.

"This is a far more interesting situation than I bargained for."

"Will you please stop that and unbutton me?" she said sharply, distrusting the amusement in his eyes.

"Certainly. As my lady requests." He stood far too close for her comfort. "Turn around and stand in the light."

She felt the back of her dress loosen as he undid the buttons, his warm fingers straying over her back and sending tingles down her spine through the thin cotton of her chemise.

He unbuttoned the dress down to her hips

and then loosened her stays with a few deft motions. She held her dress up with one hand and removed the busk from her stays with the other. She handed the polished piece of wood to him.

"Here. Hold this."

"What...? Oh, I see." He weighed the busk in his hand. "I must keep this in mind."

Pushing from the bottom of the busk pocket with one hand, she stuck her fingers in and felt around until she was able to grasp the edge of the paper. Triumphantly, she yanked it free and showed it to him.

"Good girl," he said. "But I should get you dressed first."

She re-inserted the busk and waited as he fiddled with the strings of her stays and re-buttoned her dress. She yanked her bodice back into place and turned to face him, the paper still in her hand.

"How do I know which side you're on?" she said.

"You don't, unfortunately. You will need to trust me."

She continued to hover on the edge of uncertainty, but his patience steadied her. Sir Malcolm's actions had already proven to her satisfaction he could not be trusted. If this man was working against Sir Malcolm, that was already a point in his favor. Even if ...

"What is your name?"

"Excuse me?"

"I can't give this to you until I know your real name."

His eyes searched hers and saw how important it was to her. He made her an elegant bow, with the mocking edge that was uniquely his.

"Samuel Valentine, at your service."

"Is that your real name?"

"It's the one my mother gave me, yes."

She stood irresolute until he sighed.

"Grace. I assure you we both have the same purpose—to rescue Harriet and bring her back safe and sound."

She handed over the paper, and Samuel let out a puff of breath. "Thank you."

As he scanned it, she donned and re-buttoned her spencer before joining him near the open door. She tried not to fidget as he removed a small book from his pocket and consulted it before looking at her.

"Can you ride astride?"

"If I have to," she said, blessing the fact that the skirts of this season's dresses were fuller than previous seasons.

Samuel nodded to the woods. "My horse is there. I'll run to the stables to get one for you and meet you back here."

"Where are we going?"

"The signal station at Prawle."

He left at a run, and she plunged into the woods to locate his horse. He had looped its reins to a tree branch and it raised its head to examine her, a few clovers still sticking from its mouth as she came closer. She whispered to it until it snorted and allowed her to stroke its nose. She unlooped the reins and led it back to the clearing to wait for Samuel.

The horse was a plain dark bay with one white stocking, but its eye was intelligent and it looked strong and quick. She was almost certain it was the same horse "Reverend Watkins" had ridden to their rescue … how many days ago now?

She was still whispering to the horse and counting days in her head when she heard hoofbeats pounding towards her. She looked up in alarm to see Samuel astride a piebald horse. He leaped off, shoved her into the saddle, and hastily shortened the stirrups before mounting his own horse, re-slinging the rifle against the saddle. He turned to look back at her.

"Let's go."

He nudged his horse into a fast trot. The piebald snorted but followed, and Grace let it have its head.

"How far are we going?" she called ahead.

"About fifteen miles. Hurry."

He urged his horse into a canter and, with a sigh, she followed suit. It was a long, uncomfortable, dusty ride, and Samuel pulled them up well out of sight of the signal station. He dismounted and helped her off her horse, holding her by the waist for a long moment.

"If something happens to me—no, listen, Grace! This is important." He gave her a tiny shake. "If something happens to me, I want you to go straight to the navy yard at Plymouth and ask to speak to Captain Harlowe. Did you hear me?"

"Yes."

"What did I say?"

"Plymouth. Navy. Captain Harlowe. All right?"

He relaxed and dropped his hands. "All right."

There was not much cover on the stark cliffs, but they picked their way towards the signal post in the distance until Samuel extended an arm to stop her and dropped to the ground. She followed suit and waited while he removed a small spyglass from his jacket and trained it on the area for a long moment.

He shook his head and then handed the spyglass to her.

A motionless body in the uniform of a naval lieutenant lay near the signal pole, surrounded by a dark stain. Blood. Three other men were tied hand and foot nearby with an armed man standing guard over them. Grace was almost certain she recognized him as the man who had helped search Harriet's room.

The man she knew as "Smith" stood next to the signal pole, holding a musket and scanning the water to the north. Sir Malcolm stood with him, unarmed and looking bored, but his hand hovered near the pocket of his coat in a way that made her think he still had his pistol. She did not understand the message the flags were sending, but she had to assume it was a false one given all the trouble the villains had gone to in order to access them.

Aunt Harriet sat on a rock nearby, completely composed, her gloved hands folded neatly in her lap.

Samuel bit back a curse. "Four hostages, not just one."

"What about your rifle?"

"A rifle's not much good when there are hostages at stake."

Grace lay her head down against her folded arms, and she felt one of his hands settle comfortingly on her shoulder.

"I'm not crying," she said. "I'm thinking. Where are their horses?"

He laughed softly and squeezed her shoulder. "That's my girl."

12

The sun was starting to sink in the sky and Samuel was muttering about the evening tides by the time they had worked out their plan. He had been dead set against it at first, but Grace had pointed out that, of the two of them, she was much the smaller and would be less conspicuous creeping from rock to rock to get as close to Harriet as possible. Besides, she did not know how to use the rifle and there was no time to teach her.

"All right," he said at last. "There's no more time to argue. Go."

Moving carefully and knowing her dress was already the same color as the dusty ground thanks to their frantic ride, Grace crept along a circuitous path that brought her to the edge of the cliff before working her way back towards where Harriet sat.

She was within a few yards of her aunt when hoofbeats rumbled along the ground and a horse came into view, cantering past with dragging reins.

Smith cursed volubly. "Go catch the bastard, O'Brien, or you'll be walking back to London. I'll watch the prisoners."

O'Brien put his musket aside and chased the horse while Smith looked back in the direction the animal had come from, frowning.

"What—"

A rifle shot rang out and Smith fell, dropping his musket. Grace ran forward to her aunt, who had already slid off the back of the boulder she was sitting on to take cover, but it was too late.

Sir Malcolm retrieved O'Brien's musket and pointed it at them.

"Don't be a fool," Harriet said calmly.

"She's right, Sir Malcolm," Samuel's voice called. "It's over."

Involuntarily, Sir Malcolm's head jerked in the direction of Samuel's voice, and in one smooth motion, Harriet lifted her skirt, drew out a knife, and flung it at him. It sank into his shoulder and he dropped the musket just before Samuel knocked his feet out from under him.

Harriet darted forward and retrieved the musket, whirling to point it at the returning O'Brien, who abruptly stopped and raised his hands.

"Grace," Samuel said. "Untie the sailors so they can go for help."

Two of them ran off while the other helped Samuel lower the false signal flags Smith and Sir Malcolm had raised to lure the ship carrying Napoleon into a trap.

THE LONG, boring wait for reinforcements abruptly turned into a whirlwind of activity that left Grace with a headache and a dull feeling of depression as Samuel and Harriet made glib explanation after explanation, half of which seemed to contradict what either of them had told Grace. She was not surprised when O'Brien confessed he and Smith had been the "highwaymen" who attacked her and Harriet, hoping to retrieve the brooch.

At long last they were ready to make the trip back to Lady Ridley's, Grace driving Harriet in Sir Malcolm's gig with Grace's horse tied behind and Samuel riding alongside them.

They went at a slow pace for the sake of the horses, and Grace's temper rose with every mile they traveled.

"Is she not everything I said she was?" Aunt Harriet demanded of Samuel, and he laughed.

"That she is, Harriet." He smiled at Grace, inviting her in on the joke.

She did not smile back. "How long have you known each other?"

"How long? Years and years. My dear Fillmore and I rescued him from the gallows when he was a mere child and taught him everything he knows."

"I was not actually *on* the gallows," Samuel protested.

"You would have ended there if Fillmore had not taken you in hand." Harriet turned to Grace. "Still one of the best pickpockets I've ever seen, and his acting skills—superb!"

"Yes," Grace said. "He certainly had me fooled."

Samuel shot her a puzzled look, but she ignored him. She had been a fool from the very start, and the two of them had been laughing up their sleeves at her the entire time.

"It was necessary we keep you in the dark, Grace," he said. "It was for your own safety."

"Of course," Grace ground out.

Aunt Harriet laughed again, setting Grace's teeth on edge. "You really caused no end of trouble by taking that brooch, my dear. But it all came right in the end."

"Yes, of course." Grace pulled up the horse and handed the reins to Harriet before jumping down from the gig. "Excuse me."

Samuel drew his horse to a halt and exchanged a startled glance with Harriet.

"Are you all right, my dear?" Harriet ventured.

"Why wouldn't I be? I simply need some time to myself."

"Grace …" Samuel said as he dismounted.

Grace ignored him and began stalking down the road. She had been a fool, and the two of them had made a fool of her for the last time. She was hot, and filthy, and she had seen a man killed before her eyes, and they were both acting as though it were all perfectly normal, a jolly day in the country. Angry tears pricked at her eyes, and she blinked them away.

To her further annoyance, Samuel caught up to her almost immediately. He paced alongside her in silence for what seemed like forever until she finally halted in exasperation and glared up at him, her hands clenched at her sides.

"Why don't you leave me alone?" she demanded.

"Because I think you don't understand what happened."

"Don't I? Go on. Go back to your ... your operation, or whatever you call it."

She started walking again, and he once again fell into stride next to her.

"I didn't realize what Harriet was up to at first either, Grace."

"Oh?"

"The matchmaking, I mean."

Her stumble was not graceful at all, of course—he had to grab her by the waist to prevent her from falling headlong into the noisome ditch running next to the road. And then, of course, the scoundrel neatly turned her in his arms and embraced her even though she pressed her hands against his chest so she could push him away. His warm, hard chest, where she could feel his heart beating fast even through the layers of his clothing.

"Grace, darling ..."

She refused to look at him, though her body insisted on swaying towards his with a mind of its own, eager to accept the comfort and protection he offered.

"What do you mean, matchmaking?"

"Haven't you figured it out by now?" His warm lips brushed against her temple, and she shivered. "You've guessed everything else."

Without conscious volition, her hands crept around his waist of their own accord to pull him closer, even as she kept her eyes trained on his neckcloth. Really, her body could not be trusted around him in the least, even when her mind was still urging caution.

"I can't guess," she said. "You need to say it."

She risked a glance up at him to see those strange gray-green eyes glowing down at her with a warmth that melted her resistance. "I love you. You're the bravest woman I've ever met after Harriet. Marry me, Grace."

He didn't give her time to refuse, but dipped his head to kiss her, and she couldn't stop herself from kissing him back. Not even the rattle of the gig disturbed them—Aunt Harriet had to clear her throat three times before Samuel finally pulled back.

"Well, children?" Harriet said. "Is it settled?"

Samuel looked down at Grace. "Is it settled?"

"You're both mad," Grace said. "And you've clearly turned me into a Bedlamite as well. Yes. I'll marry you."

"Oh, my dears, how I've missed you!"

Grace watched from the doorstep of their cottage as Samuel handed first Aunt Harriet and then Parker down from their carriage.

"Hello, aunt," Grace said, returning her aunt's embrace and peck on the cheek. "How was your journey?"

"Oh, dreadful, of course. The roads were as bad as ever. But Parker and I kept our spirits up, didn't we?"

Parker made a small noise that might have passed as a snort and marched up the walkway to the door of the cottage as Samuel followed behind, Aunt Harriet's small trunk perched on his shoulder. He waggled his eyebrows at Grace as he walked by, and she restrained a snicker as he followed Parker up the stairs to the guest bedroom.

Aunt Harriet looked around the entryway of the cottage with a pleased smile on her face. "I have to admit, I was skeptical when Samuel announced his decision to retire to Kent and live in rural obscurity, but this is quite lovely."

"Thank you," Grace murmured, leading her aunt to the large parlor, which overlooked the garden at the back of the cottage.

"I approve," Harriet said. "Does Samuel do the gardening?"

"No, we have hired a local man to take care of it." As Harriet settled herself on the settee, Grace crossed to the bellpull and rang for the housekeeper. She must have been waiting with everything ready, for the parlor door opened only a few minutes later as the housekeeper entered with a tray laden with tea and delicacies.

"Thank you, Mrs. Kilson," Grace murmured. "Would you be so kind as to see if Parker requires any refreshments as well?"

Mrs. Kilson curtsied, cast one more curious glance at Harriet, and exited the room just as Samuel came in.

"She's all settled," he said cheerfully, making a proper bow to Harriet as she beamed at him.

"You look very well, Samuel," Harriet said,

and cast a sly glance at Grace. "Married life agrees with you."

"Very well, indeed," he said with a smile as he settled onto the settee next to Grace and squeezed her hand. She knew her grin was idiotically doting, but so was his.

When she looked over at Harriet, the older woman had a look of smug satisfaction.

"You know that I hate to say that I told you so—"

"You love to say 'I told you so,'" Grace said.

"—but I knew you two would suit. I just knew it."

Grace smiled and gave up. When Harriet was determined to say something, no power on heaven or earth could stop her.

As Grace poured the tea, they made conversation about Harriet's journey and the latest developments with the new treaty with France until they each began their second cup of tea. Harriet took one sip and set her cup down with a clink.

"Tell me, Grace—any sign yet that you are increasing?"

Samuel choked and sputtered as his sip of tea went the wrong way, and Grace hoped that the process of patting his back would disguise her blush. They had discussed their mutual desire to postpone parenthood for at least a year or two, and the delightful and increasingly inventive methods of preventing pregnancy that Samuel had shown her had occupied much of their time since the wedding.

"No," Grace said, focusing her attention on the tea tray. "I do not believe there is."

Harriet nodded. "Very good. You see, I must confess to having an ... ulterior motive for my visit."

"You don't say," Samuel murmured, and Harriet glared at him.

"There is no need to be pert with me, my dear. But when your country calls, you really ought to answer."

Samuel sent a reassuring glance to Grace and then focused on Harriet. "My country ought to know better than to try and contact me while I am still honeymooning."

Harriet waved any airy hand. "But it's nearly the end of October, Samuel, dear. You should be well past the honeymoon by now."

Samuel only smiled, and this time it was Harriet who blushed a little.

"Well, as you would know if you read the messages that had been sent to you," Harriet said, "there has been some unrest in France surrounding the restoration of the Bourbons and the renegotiation of the treaty. Whitehall would like for us to review the situation and report back."

"Us?"

"Well, of course. All of us." Harriet smiled her most vivacious smile. "After all, I am the most senior agent of all of us." The smile dimmed a bit. "And I have missed you, my dears. Truly."

Samuel turned to Grace. "Well?"

"Well?"

After a fraught moment, Grace was unable to repress her giggle for a moment longer. Harriet frowned between them as Samuel, too, burst into laughter.

"You dreadful children," she said. "You intended to say yes all along!"

As Samuel laughed, he tugged Grace close with an arm around her shoulders. "Grace has been in training since we received the first message. She is still not quite as good with a knife as you, but she is a crack shot with a pistol and can toss me to the ground if I don't watch myself when we spar."

A slow smile crossed Harriet's face. "Well, then. What are we waiting for?"

ACKNOWLEDGMENTS

The original version of this story was my first published work of fiction, so I want to thank the author collective that is New Romance Café Publishing—including Andie Wood, Anna Volkin, Jenny Simon, Shanti Mercer, and Sofia Aves—for taking a chance on me and letting me call a 20,000-word novella a "short story." My fellow author Caro Kincaid was my beta reader, and has been helping me with that ever since. Whitney Jones at Empowered Writing did a line edit, but also gave me a few developmental notes and some Deep Thoughts about the genre that made me giggle. And I will always thank my husband, who supports me in all ways, even when I say things like, *I think I want to start writing romance novels*.

ABOUT THE AUTHOR

Alexa Santi has been fascinated by the Regency Era since the pre-internet days when she had to check paper books out from the library. It took some time for her to settle on fiction after several detours, including an MFA in screenwriting. She lives in Los Angeles with her handsome archivist husband and their pesky cats, who insist she take frequent breaks from her writing to pay attention to them. You can find her on Facebook, Instagram, or on her website, https://www.alexasanti.com